One-Eye! Two-Eyes! Three-Eyes!

For my sister, Pamela

—A. S.

For Gill, Sarah, and Ben

—G. C.

Atheneum Books for Young Readers
An imprint of Simon & Schuster Children's Publishing Division
1230 Avenue of the Americas
New York, New York 10020
Text copyright © 2007 by Aaron Shepard
Illustrations copyright © 2007 by Gary Clement
All rights reserved, including the right of reproduction in whole or in part in any form.
Book design by Sonia Chaghatzbanian
The text for this book is set in Centaur.
The illustrations for this book are rendered in watercolor and pencil.
Manufactured in China
First Edition
2 4 6 8 10 9 7 5 3 1
Library of Congress Cataloging-in-Publication Data
Shepard, Aaron.
One-eye! Two-eyes! Three-eyes! a very Grimm fairy tale/Aaron Shepard;
illustrated by Gary Clement.—1st ed.
p.   cm.
Summary: A retelling of a classic fairy tale about a little girl who has two eyes
and is horribly teased by her sisters who have one and three eyes respectively.
ISBN-13: 978-0-689-86740-8
ISBN-10: 0-689-86740-9
[1. Fairy tales. 2. Folklore.] I. Clement, Gary, ill.
II. Title: One Eye, Two Eyes, Three Eyes. English. III. Title.
PZ8.S3425Two 2007
398.2—dc22   2005000459

told by Aaron Shepard

One-Eye!

pictures by Gary Clement

Two-Eyes!

Three-Eyes!

A Very Grimm Fairy Tale

ATHENEUM BOOKS FOR YOUNG READERS

NEW YORK   LONDON   TORONTO   SYDNEY

nce there were three sisters who lived together in a cottage in the woods. They had been there for as long as they could remember, and they never saw anyone else.

Now, the oldest sister was no different from other people. Her name was One-Eye. She had just one eye, right in the middle of her forehead.

The middle sister was also quite ordinary. Her name was Three-Eyes. She had one eye on her forehead, and one on each side of her face.

But the youngest sister was *different*. Her name was Two-Eyes, and that's just what she had.

Because Two-Eyes was not like the others, her older sisters were ashamed of her and picked on her all the time. They dressed her in ragged hand-me-downs and only let her eat leftovers.

Now, the sisters owned a goat, and every day Two-Eyes took it to the meadow to graze. One morning, when she'd had hardly anything to eat, she sat on the grass and cried her two eyes out.

All at once, an old woman stood before her. But the biggest surprise was that this woman had two eyes, just like Two-Eyes herself.

"What's wrong, my dear?" asked the woman.

"It's my sisters," Two-Eyes told her. "They never give me enough to eat."

"Don't worry about that!" said the woman. "You can have as much as you like. Just say to your goat,

'Bleat, goat, bleat.
And bring me lots to eat!'

Then you'll have plenty. When you don't want any more, just say,

'Bleat, goat, bleat.
I've had so much to eat!'

Then the rest will vanish. Just like this."

And the old woman vanished—just like that.

Two-Eyes couldn't wait to try. She said to the goat,

"Bleat, goat, bleat.
And bring me lots to eat!"

The goat bleated, and a little table and chair appeared. The table was set with a tablecloth, plate, and silverware, and on it were dishes and dishes of wonderful-smelling food.

"This sure is better than leftovers!" said Two-Eyes.

She sat down and started in hungrily. Everything tasted delicious. When she'd eaten her fill, she said,

"Bleat, goat, bleat.
I've had so much to eat!"

The goat bleated, and the table vanished. "And *that*," said Two-Eyes, "is better than cleaning up!"

When Two-Eyes got home, she didn't touch her bowl of leftovers. Her sisters didn't notice till she'd gone off to bed. Then Three-Eyes said, "Look! Our little sister didn't eat anything!"

"That's strange," said One-Eye. "Is someone else giving her food? I'll go tomorrow and watch her."

The next morning, when Two-Eyes started out, One-Eye said, "I'm coming along to make sure you tend the goat properly." Then she followed Two-Eyes to the meadow and kept a careful eye on her. So Two-Eyes never got to use the old woman's rhyme.

When they got home, Two-Eyes ate her bowl of leftovers. Then she went off to the woods and cried her two eyes out.

The old woman appeared again.

"What's wrong, my dear?"

"It's my sisters. The goat can't bring me food, because One-Eye is watching me."

"Don't worry about that!" said the woman. "You can stop her if you like. Just sing her this song.

> 'Is your eye awake?
> Is your eye asleep?
> Is your eye awake?
> Is your eye asleep?'

Keep singing that, and she'll sleep soon enough."

Then the old woman vanished.

The next morning, when Two-Eyes went to the meadow, One-Eye again went along. Two-Eyes said, "Sister, let me sing to you." And she sang to her over and over,

> "Is your eye awake?
> Is your eye asleep?
> Is your eye awake?
> Is your eye asleep?"

One-Eye's eyelid began to droop, and soon she was fast asleep. Then Two-Eyes said to the goat,

> "Bleat, goat, bleat.
> And bring me lots to eat!"

The goat bleated, the table appeared, and Two-Eyes ate her fill. Then she said,

> "Bleat, goat, bleat.
> I've had so much to eat!"

The goat bleated again, and the table vanished. Then Two-Eyes shook her sister, saying, "Wake up, sleepyhead!"

When they got home, Two-Eyes didn't touch her leftovers. After she'd gone off to bed, Three-Eyes asked, "What happened?"

"How should I know?" said One-Eye. "I fell asleep. If you think you can do better, then you go tomorrow."

So the next morning, when Two-Eyes went to the meadow, Three-Eyes went along and kept *three* careful eyes on her. "Listen," said Two-Eyes, "and I'll sing to you." And she sang to her over and over,

"Is your eye awake?
Is your eye asleep?
Is your eye awake?
Is your eye asleep?"

As Two-Eyes sang, the eye on her sister's forehead went to sleep—but her other two eyes didn't! Three-Eyes pretended, though, by closing them *almost* all the way and peeking through. She couldn't quite hear what Two-Eyes told the goat, but she saw everything.

That night, when Two-Eyes had gone off to bed, One-Eye asked, "What happened?"

"Our sister knows a charm to make the goat bring wonderful food," said Three-Eyes. "But I couldn't hear the words."

"Then let's get rid of the goat," said One-Eye. And they drove it off into the woods.

The next morning, One-Eye told Two-Eyes, "You thought you could eat better than your sisters, did you? Well, the goat is gone, so that's that."

Two-Eyes went down to the stream and cried her two eyes out. Again the old woman appeared. "What's wrong, my dear?"

"It's my sisters. The song didn't work on Three-Eyes. She saw everything, and now they've chased away the goat."

"Silly girl! That charm was just for One-Eye. For Three-Eyes, you should have sung,

> 'Are your eyes awake?
> Are your eyes asleep?'

But don't worry about that. Here, take this seed and plant it in front of your cottage. You'll soon have a tall tree with leaves of silver and apples of gold. When you want an apple, just say,

> 'Apple hanging on the tree,
> I am Two-Eyes. Come to me!'

It will fall right into your hand."

Again the old woman vanished. Two-Eyes went home and waited till her sisters weren't looking, then dug a small hole and planted the seed.

The next morning a tall tree stood before the cottage with leaves of silver and apples of gold. Two-Eyes found her sisters gaping at it in astonishment.

All at once Three-Eyes cried, "Look! A man!"
Riding toward them was a knight in full armor, his visor over his face.

"Quick!" said One-Eye. "Hide our little sister!" So they lowered an empty barrel over Two-Eyes.

"Good morning, ladies," the knight said as he rode up. "Beautiful tree you have there. I would dearly love to have one of those apples. In fact, I would grant anything in my power to the lady who first gave me one."

The two sisters gasped. They scrambled over to the tree and jumped up and down, trying to grab the apples. But the branches just lifted themselves higher, so the apples were always out of reach.

Meanwhile Two-Eyes raised her barrel just a little and kicked a stone so that it rolled over to the knight.

"That's odd," he said. "That stone seems to have come from that barrel. Does anyone happen to be in there?"

"Oh no, sir," said One-Eye, "not really. Just our little sister."

"She's *different*," said Three-Eyes, "so we can't let anyone see her."

"But I *want* to see her," said the knight. "Young lady, please come out!"

So Two-Eyes lifted off the barrel.

"My word!" said the knight. "She's the loveliest young lady I've ever seen!" He raised his visor for a better look.

"Oh no!" screamed One-Eye and
Three-Eyes together. *"Two eyes!"*
Sure enough, the knight had two eyes,
just like their sister.

"Dear lady," said the knight, "can *you* give me
an apple from that tree?"

"Of course!" said Two-Eyes. Standing under it,
she said,

"Apple hanging on the tree,
I am Two-Eyes. Come to me!"

An apple dropped right into her hand, and she
gave it to the knight.

"My thanks," he said. "And now I will grant
you anything in my power."

"Well, to start with," said Two-Eyes, "you can
take me away from these horrid, hateful sisters!"

So the knight took Two-Eyes back to his castle. And since they had so much in common—after all, they both had two eyes—you can be sure they lived happily ever after.

MUSIC FOR
Four Hands
and Eyes

As for One-Eye and Three-Eyes, day after day they stood under that tree and repeated their sister's words.

"Apple hanging on the tree,
I am Two-Eyes. Come to me!"

But the apples never fell for them, and they never did figure out why.

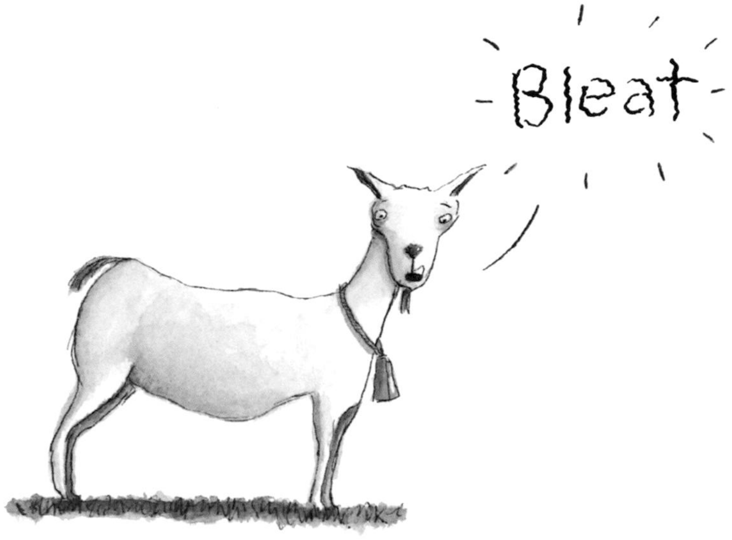
Bleat

About the Story

For the old woman's sleeping song, any tune will work, but here's the one she taught Two-Eyes.

Is your eye a - wake? Is your eye a - sleep?

Ever have trouble sleeping? Then you can use the song on yourself! Just be sure to say the right words. Here they are, for anyone with two or more eyes.

Are my eyes awake?

Are my eyes asleep?

To hear the tune, and for a reader's theater script of this story, visit my home page at www.aaronshep.com.

This telling is based loosely on "One-Eye, Two-Eyes, and Three-Eyes," number 130 in the tales of the Brothers Grimm.

—*Aaron Shepard*